Max rides his bike

Story by Jenny Giles
Illustrations by Richard Hoit

Max said to Grandpa,

"I can ride my bike like this.

Can the little wheels come off?"

Grandpa looked at Max's bike.

"The little wheels can come off

your bike today," he said.

Grandpa said,

"Look at your bike, Max.

No little wheels!"

Max got on his bike.

He went for a little ride

on the grass.

Max came down

on the grass.

The bike came down on Max!

Grandpa said,
"The little wheels can go
back on your bike."

"No, Grandpa," said Max.
"I am going to ride my bike
with **no** little wheels."

"I will help you," said Grandpa.

"No, Grandpa," said Max.
"I can ride my bike like this."

Max got back on his bike.

Max went for a ride
on his bike.
He went up and down
on the grass.

"Grandpa! Look at me!"
shouted Max.

"No little wheels!"